First published in 2004 by
Franklin Watts
96 Leonard Street
London
EC2A 4XD

Franklin Watts Australia
45–51 Huntley Street
Alexandria
NSW 2015

A CIP catalogue record for this book is available
from the British Library.

ISBN 0 7496 5737 5 (hbk)
ISBN 0 7496 5775 8 (pbk)

Series Editor: Jackie Hamley
Series Advisors: Dr Barrie Wade, Dr Hilary Minns
Design: Peter Scoulding

Printed in Hong Kong / China

For Alicia with love – MN

The Fox
and
the Stork

Retold by
Margaret Nash

Illustrated by
Richard Morgan

W
FRANKLIN WATTS
LONDON•SYDNEY

Margaret Nash

"Foxes visit my garden. They eat any food scraps they find. Perhaps I should make them some soup!"

Richard Morgan

"I hope you enjoy the pictures in this book and get to slurp lots of soup with your friends!"

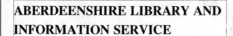

One day, greedy Fox asked
Stork to dinner.

"Mmm," said Fox.
"This soup is good.
Do you like it,
Stork?"

"I can't eat it," said poor
Stork. "The dish is too flat
for my beak."

Greedy Fox ate Stork's soup, too!

9

Stork went home hungry.

Then she had an idea.

Stork asked Fox to dinner.

12

13

"Mmm," said Stork.
"This soup is great!
Do you like it, Fox?"

14

15

"I can't eat it," said Fox.
"The jug is too narrow
for my nose."

17

"Poor you!" said Stork, and she ate up Fox's dinner.

19

Fox ran home hungry.

21

But he wasn't so greedy
the next time Stork
came to dinner!

23

Notes for parents and teachers

READING CORNER has been structured to provide maximum support for new readers. The stories may be used by adults for sharing with young children. Primarily, however, the stories are designed for newly independent readers, whether they are reading these books in bed at night, or in the reading corner at school or in the library.

Starting to read alone can be a daunting prospect. READING CORNER helps by providing visual support and repeating words and phrases, while making reading enjoyable. These books will develop confidence in the new reader, and encourage a love of reading that will last a lifetime!

If you are reading this book with a child, here are a few tips:

1. Make reading fun! Choose a time to read when you and the child are relaxed and have time to share the story.

2. Encourage children to reread the story, and to retell the story in their own words, using the illustrations to remind them what has happened.

3. Give praise! Remember that small mistakes need not always be corrected.

READING CORNER covers three grades of early reading ability, with three levels at each grade. Each level has a certain number of words per story, indicated by the number of bars on the spine of the book, to allow you to choose the right book for a young reader:

GRADE 1	GRADE 2	GRADE 3
50 words	130 words	250 words
70 words	160 words	350 words
100 words	200 words	450 words